Abby the Acrocat

Written by
Alan Durant

Illustrated by
Amy Bradley

Abby's family were all burglars.
Her pa, Alfred, was a burglar.
Her ma, Annie, was a thief.
Her brothers, Arthur and 'Arry, stole things too.

Her uncle, Arnold, was a robber.
Even her grandpa Albert was a burglar (but he had retired).

Abby was not a burglar. Her dad said that she was too small.

"You have to be strong too, to carry all the swag," he told Abby.

"*And* you have to be able to leap very high and run very fast," added Annie.

"Like us," purred Arthur and 'Arry.

"I can do that," said Abby crossly. "Anyway, who wants to be a burglar? All you do is creep into houses and steal things. Robbing's wrong."

"What a thing to say!" tutted Uncle Arnold. "We aren't *just* burglars. We're the best burglars in the business."

"Hear hear!" muttered Grandpa Albert. Then he fell asleep.

"When's our next job, pa?" asked 'Arry.

"Tonight," said Alfred. "We're going to Mog Street."

Alfred showed them the plans.

Mog Street Burglary

Alfred's swag = silk scarves

Annie's swag = balls of wool

Arnold's swag = soft toys (no dogs!)

Arthur's swag = furry slippers

'Arry's swag = fish fingers

Late that night, when the moon was out, Abby's family went to work.

Abby's job was to look after the swag cart.
"Make sure no one steals it," laughed Arthur.

Abby had to wait a long time. She soon got bored. She decided to practise her acrobatics while she waited.

She flipped up onto a wall and balanced on one paw.

She danced on the telephone wire.

She spun and she twirled.

She jumped in the air, turned head over heels and made a perfect landing on all four paws.

Then she bowed.

Arnold was the first to come back, dragging a giant teddy.

"Help me with this, Abby," he puffed.

One by one the others returned and the cart was filled up with swag.

Abby's brothers pushed her out of the way.

"You're too small to pull the cart," they laughed.

Abby was very cross.

Back home, Abby's family had a party. Abby sat in a corner and scowled.

"Cheer up, Abby. One day you can be a burglar too," said Uncle Arnold.

"I don't want to be a burglar," said Abby crossly. "Robbing's wrong."

Everyone laughed at Abby.

After a while, Abby's family went to bed. But not Abby.

She had a plan. *I'll show them*, she thought.

Abby pulled the full swag cart out of the house and all the way back to Mog Street.

One by one, she took the swag off the cart and put it back where it had come from.

She climbed up pipes, she jumped on walls, she swung on window sills and she slinked through tiny openings.

It was hard work, but at last it was done. Everything was back in its right place.

On her way home, Abby saw something interesting:

"Hmm," she said to herself, and she took the poster.

The next morning, Abby was woken up by a terrible yowling.

"Someone's stolen our swag!" cried Alfred.

"Rotten robbers," said Annie.

"Yowl!" went Abby's brothers.

"Snore!" went Grandpa Albert.

"Whoever could it be?" said Uncle Arnold.

"It was me!" said Abby, and she told them all what she'd done.

"But why?" they asked.

"To show you that I can do all the things you can do," said Abby.

"You want to be a burglar like us?" said Alfred proudly.

Abby shook her head. "I don't want to be a burglar. Robbing's wrong. I want to be an acrobat!"

Abby showed them the circus poster.

"I've always wanted to be in the circus," said Annie.

"Me too," said Arthur.

"Me three," said 'Arry.

"It does look like fun," said Uncle Arnold.

"I suppose robbing *is* wrong," said Alfred. "Maybe it's time we put our skills to good use."

"Hear, hear!" said Grandpa Albert in his sleep.

So, that very day, Abby and her family joined the circus.

Now none of Abby's family is a burglar. They are all acrobats. They are *the best* acrobats in the business. They make people laugh and gasp and clap.

And best of them all, topping the bill and stealing the show, is Abby, the acrocat!